To Christopher Sebastian Charles,
the universe is better with you in it. — T.C.

I dedicate this book as a visual love note of welcome to
all the children and their families on the planet here today,
and to those who have yet to arrive. — B.C.

Text copyright © 2020 by Tami Charles • Illustrations copyright © 2020 by Bryan Collier • All rights reserved. Published by Orchard Books, an imprint of Scholastic Inc., *Publishers since 1920.* • ORCHARD BOOKS and design are registered trademarks of Watts Publishing Group, Ltd., used under license. SCHOLASTIC and associated logos are trademarks and/or registered trademarks of Scholastic Inc. • The publisher does not have any control over and does not assume any responsibility for author or third-party websites or their content. • No part of this publication may be reproduced, stored in a retrieval system, or transmitted in any form or by any means, electronic, mechanical, photocopying, recording, or otherwise, without written permission of the publisher. For information regarding permission, write to Scholastic Inc., Attention: Permissions Department, 557 Broadway, New York, NY 10012. • This book is a work of fiction. Names, characters, places, and incidents are either the product of the author's imagination or are used fictitiously, and any resemblance to actual persons, living or dead, business establishments, events, or locales is entirely coincidental. • Library of Congress Cataloging-in-Publication Data available ISBN 978-1-338-57485-2 • 10 9 8 7 6 5 4 3 2 1   20 21 22 23 24 • Printed in China 38 • First edition, October 2020
Book design by Rae Crawford • The art for this book was created with collage and Winsor & Newton watercolor paint on 300lb. Arches watercolor paper.

ALL BECAUSE YOU MATTER

Written by
Tami Charles

Illustrated by
Caldecott Honor Winner
Bryan Collier

Orchard Books

New York
an imprint of Scholastic Inc.

They say that matter
is all things
that make up the universe:
energy,

stars,

space . . .

If that's the case,
then you, dear child, matter.

Long before you took
your place in this world,
you were dreamed of,
like a knapsack
full of wishes,
carried on the backs
of your ancestors
as they created
empires,
pyramids,
legacies.

Building,
   inventing,
      working
beneath red-hot suns
and cold-blue moons,
thinking of you,
years ahead.
Because to them,
you always mattered.

On the night you were born,
stars sprayed across the sky,
each one full of
    light,
      hope,
        love,
and all the moments
in your life that would matter . . .

Like your first steps,
bare feet planted on
cold floor,
hobbling,
wobbling,
toppling,
only to stand
and try again.

Or your first words,
spoken almost like a lullaby,
notes climbing a ladder to
the sky . . .
 Mamá!
  Papá!
   Mahal kita!

Or the first time you opened
a book,
like a mirror staring back at you,
and *really* saw yourself . . .
 same hair,
  same skin,
   same dreams.

The words and pictures
coming together like
sweet jam on toast,
música blasting through barrios,
sun in blue sky . . .
all because you matter.

But in galaxies far away,
it may seem that
light does not always reach
lonely planets,
covered moons,
stars unseen,
as if matter no longer exists.

And just like moons
hidden in the dark,
there will be times
when you, too,
will question your place
in the universe.
Like the time you'll hear
the teacher call your name:

Hossam

Uzoamaka

Yordenis . . .

and the whispers
and giggles begin,
followed by:
What kind of name is that?

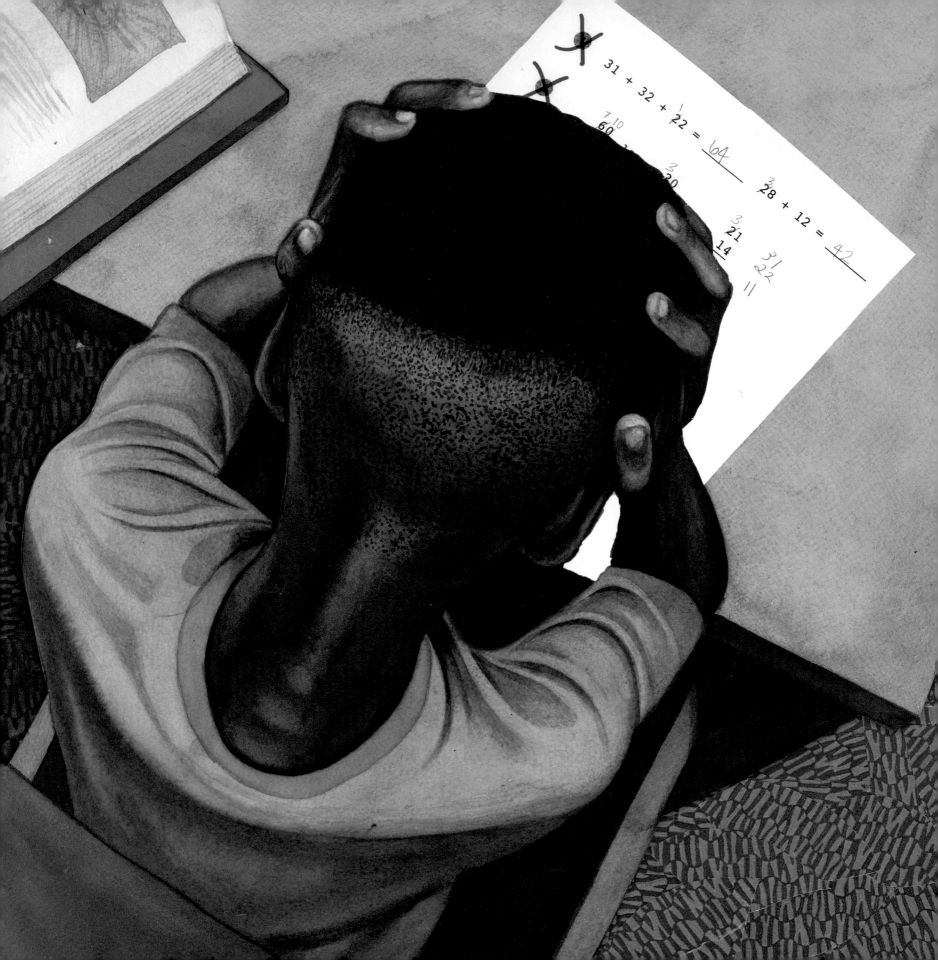

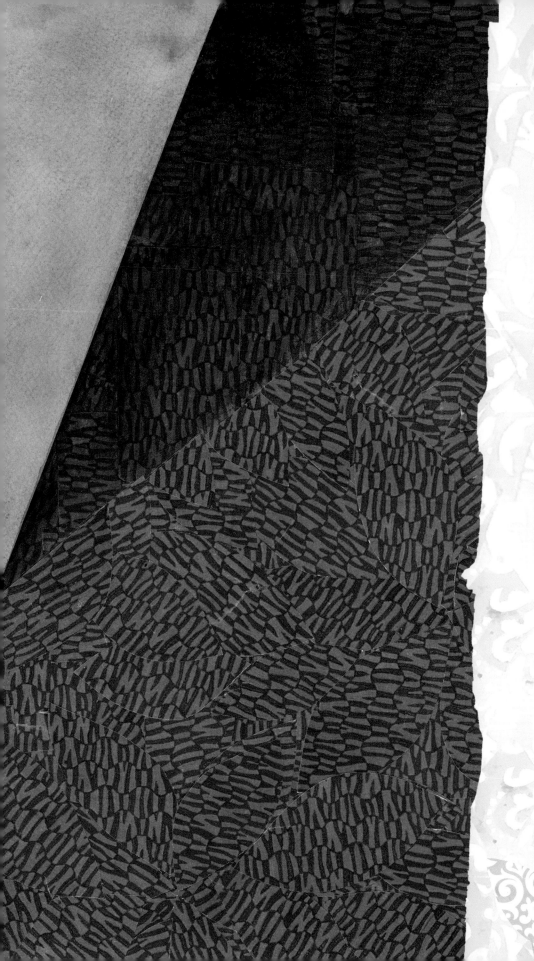

Or the time you'll see
a letter,
big,
bold,
red on the page,
and you will question
if you,
and your work,
and your effort
matter.

Or the time when your Pop Pop
turns on the news,
and you see people everywhere
take a breath,
take a stand,
take a knee.

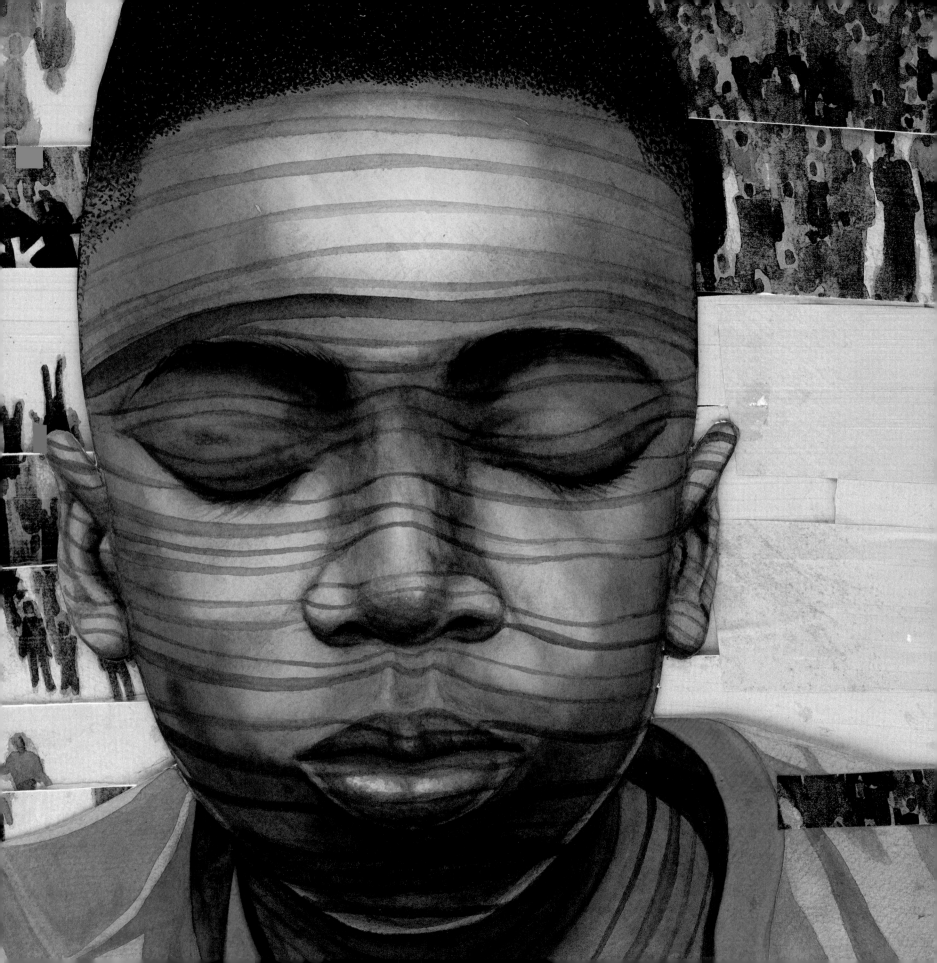

And you hear Pop Pop's
whispered prayers,
as another name is called:
Trayvon,
Tamir,
Philando,
and you wonder
if they,
or you,
will ever matter.

But did you know
that you do?

Did you know that
you were born from
       queens,
          chiefs,
             legends?

Did you know that
you are the earth?
That strength, power, and
beauty lie within you?

Did you know
that you are sun rays,
calm, like ocean waves,
tough, like montañas,
magic, like stars in space?

And on the day
the universe was created,
you were thought of,
dreamed of,
carried like a
knapsack full of wishes,
as planets,
    stars,
       moons
          took their places . . .
Making room for you,
    your people,
      their dreams,
        your future.
All because,
since the beginning of time . . .

You mattered.

They mattered.

We matter . . .

and always will.

AUTHOR'S NOTE

On the day my son, Christopher Sebastian, was born, he became the center of my universe. Sun-kissed skin, dreamy brown eyes, and a gentle "coo" that could turn me into a human puddle. Ever since his birth, it has been my greatest wish to hold him in the space of first steps, first words, first books. But time waits for no one.

As Christopher grew, so grew my own fears as a mother. I wanted to keep my little boy shielded from the cruelties of the world. But whenever I would turn on the news, I would see the same story line repeated as countless young Black men and women were taken away too soon.

In my son's early years, it was easy to avoid discussing the injustices against people of color. But soon, the questions came: Why did they assassinate Dr. King? Why won't you let me play with my Nerf guns outside? Time was up.

I knew I needed to have The Big Talk with my son. The one where I tell him that while there are many nice people in the world, not everyone is. And that sometimes people will treat others unfairly because of their skin color, race, or religion.

I wrote *All Because You Matter* to provide parents with a starting point for conversations about the racial climate in our country today. These are issues that should be discussed in all families, of all backgrounds, if we are to raise empathetic future leaders.

I also wrote this book to remind all children, especially those from marginalized backgrounds, that no matter where they come from, they matter. That the people who came before them, and the work that they did to secure the life we have today, matter. Because of this, our children must continue that work and carry themselves with pride, even when they experience moments in which they are made to feel unimportant.

I will not raise Christopher to walk in fear. And while I don't have the answers for how we can "fix" racial injustice, I can begin with this book — a loving tribute to the greatness that lives within my beautiful, brown-hued, brown-eyed boy and within all children, of all colors, everywhere . . . YOU MATTER!

ILLUSTRATOR'S NOTE

This project is a wonderful journey of promise and empowerment for our children, one that zooms through time and space. We start with a young couple anticipating the birth of a child, and then see them raise, love, and carefully guide that child through life with reassurance and a powerful sense of significance. It explores the duty we have as parents, caregivers, and world citizens to bestow love and value on our children and loved ones.

I was partly raised by my grandmother, who was a quilt maker. When you see my art, you can see her influence, as I join collage and petal shapes together to make a whole idea or image. To visually tell this story, I started with the shape of a single flower petal to build a blossoming effect in all backgrounds — like the night sky, interior wallpaper, and the child's storybook. Faces appear on those petals, representing the voices of ancestors chanting: "You matter." As our main character is faced with navigating today's challenges of identity, self-worth, survival, and the ability to thrive, he is surrounded by a community of family.